SIXTEEN COWS

Lisa Wheeler

Kurt Cyrus

N C.

ndon

For Glen, may we always moo *in unison.*
Love—L. W.

Text copyright © 2002 by Lisa Wheeler
Illustrations copyright © 2002 by Kurt Cyrus

Requests for permission to make copies of any part of the work should be
mailed to the following address: Permissions Department, Harcourt, Inc.,
6277 Sea Harbor Drive, Orlando, Florida 32887-6777.

www.HarcourtBooks.com

First Voyager Books edition 2006

Voyager Books is a trademark of Harcourt, Inc., registered in the United States of America
and/or other jurisdictions.

The Library of Congress has cataloged the hardcover edition as follows:
Wheeler, Lisa, 1963–
Sixteen cows/by Lisa Wheeler; illustrated by Kurt Cyrus.
p. cm.
Summary: Rhyming tale of Cowboy Gene and Cowgirl Sue, whose beloved cows
get mixed up when a storm blows down the fence between their ranches.
[1. Cowboys—Fiction.   2. Cowgirls—Fiction.   3. Cows—Fiction.
4. Stories in rhyme.]   I. Cyrus, Kurt, ill.   II. Title.
PZ8.3.W5668Si   2002
[E]—dc21   00-11157
ISBN-13: 978-0152-02676-9   ISBN-10: 0-15-202676-2
ISBN-13: 978-0152-05592-9 pb   ISBN-10: 0-15-205592-4 pb

H G F E D C B A

Display lettering by Tom Seibert.
The text type was set in Weiss.
Color separations by Bright Arts Ltd., Hong Kong
Printed and bound by Tien Wah Press, Singapore
Production supervision by Ginger Boyer
Designed by Judythe Sieck

Cowboy Gene was long and lean,
hair of red and eyes of green.
Loved all the cows on Biddle Ranch
and every time he got the chance,

he'd call their names out loud and strong.
Here's Gene Biddle's come-home song:

"Mudskipper! Sissy Nell! Sassafras! Mazie Bell!
Twinkle Toes! Honeydew! Buttercup! Suzy Q!"

The Biddle cows all answered, "Moo."

Cowgirl Sue was smart and true,
hair of gold and eyes of blue.
Loved all the cows on Waddle Ranch
and every time she got the chance
she'd call their names out loud and strong.

Here's Sue Waddle's come-home song:

"Sunflower! Baby Face! Button Eyes! Charlotte Grace!
Jelly Roll! Peekaboo! Cinderbox! Bobbie Lou!"

The Waddle cows all answered, "Moo," too.

Now, Waddle Ranch was on a hill and sat right next to Biddle.
And where each ranch's pasture met, a fence ran down the middle.
So Biddle cows and Waddle cows were not in any danger
of getting mixed at grazing time and dining with a stranger.

Until, just after winter thaw,
a wind blew down from Arkansas.

It skipped the barns, it skipped the hay,
but blew that fence plumb clean away.

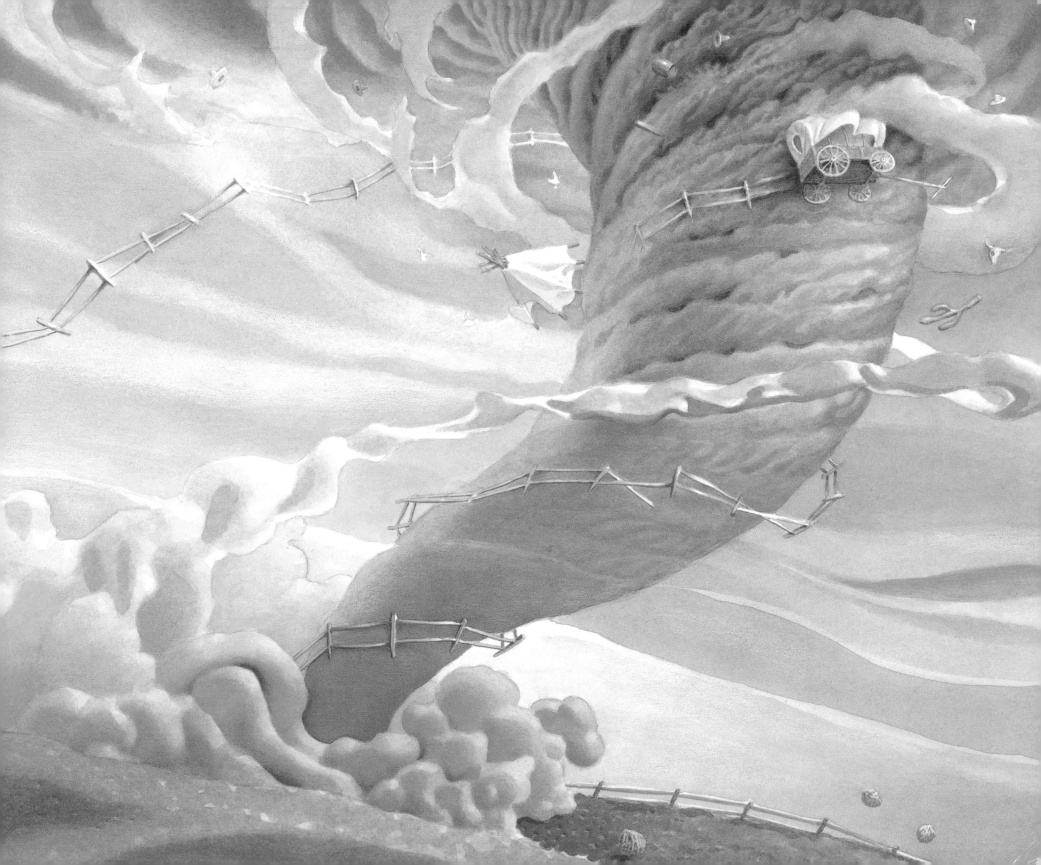

Then Biddle cows and Waddle cows were free to roam and wander.
And Cowgirl Sue, up on the hill, saw all her herd down yonder.

"Don't mingle with those low-down cows," she cried. "That just won't do!"
She broke into her come-home song…

...but Gene was singing, too.

"Sun-Skipper! Sissy-Face! Sassy-Eyes! Mazing-Grace!
Jelly-Toes! Honey-Boo! Butter-Box! Bobbie-Q!"

Cowboy Gene got hoppin' mad. "You're messin' up my song!"
Cowgirl Sue was hoppin', too. "You made me sing it wrong!"

"I'm singin' all my cows back home!"
"I'm singin' mine home, too!"

And sixteen cows in unison responded with a "MOO!"

The cows all did the two-step, as Gene commenced to singin'.
They trotted down to Biddle Ranch, their cowbells just a-ringin'!

Cowgirl Sue, at Waddle Ranch, this really got her goat.
So, when her cows had run to Gene, she opened up her throat.

The cows all did the polka, as Sue commenced to singin'.
They trotted up to Waddle Ranch, their cowbells just a-ringin'!

Sixteen cows together, ran up the hill and down.
Sixteen cows could not decide which was the sweeter sound.

This went on throughout the day, purt' near into night.

Sixteen cows ran up and down. (In truth, cows aren't too bright.)

Then Cowboy Gene took off his hat. He waved and hollered, "Stop!
If we keep up this singin' feud, our cows are sure to drop!"

"Sure enough!" Sue Waddle said, and headed down to Biddle.
Where did those ranchers call a truce? Why, smack-dab in the middle!

Gene mumbled, "What nice cows you have."
Sue blushed. "I like yours, too.
Together they're one happy herd."
And sixteen cows said, "Moo."

Come that fall, those two cowpokes exchanged their wedding vows.
Who served as honored bridesmaids? No less than sixteen cows!

Mudskipper, Baby Face, Sassafras, Charlotte Grace,
Sunflower, Sissy Nell, Button Eyes, Mazie Bell,
Twinkle Toes, Peekaboo, Buttercup, Suzy Q,
Jelly Roll, Honeydew, Cinderbox, and Bobbie Lou!

Now, when Gene sings home the cows, he sings with Cowgirl Sue,
A sound that blends together, a sound both sweet and new…

…And sixteen cows in unison come runnin' with a "MOO!"